STAY

A NOVELLA

COYOTE GRAY JR

For my beloved, Margaret Gray,
who notices before anyone else knows there is something to notice,
and adjusts the world accordingly.

For those who are afraid of spiders.
This will not help.

ONE

THE KINGDOM OF CORNERS

All of my spiders have names and backstories.

In the corners of my old house, where dust bunnies dance like tiny drunk ballerinas, I keep a secret menagerie of spiders. They're not pets. They're eccentric tenants who pay rent in fly corpses and midnight drama. Each has a name, a history, and a personality louder than a mariachi band at closing time.

I did not plan this. Nobody plans to become a landlord of arachnids. It happens the way most peculiar arrangements happen: slowly, then all at once, and by the time you realize what you've agreed to, someone has already moved furniture in and is complaining about the draft.

Under the kitchen cabinet, in the dim cathedral of spilled coffee grounds and forgotten crumbs, reigns Ethel Merman. She's a plump little orb-weaver with legs like a Broadway chorus line. Ethel sings. Not delicate chirps, not the polite hum of a background extra, but full-throated, belt-it-to-the-cheap-seats arias at three in the morning. She drinks, too. Sips from the thimble-sized drops of merlot I spill when I'm feeling dramatic, and once upon a time, she could turn the air a particular shade of blue with her vocabulary. She's been married six times, all of them disasters, the most recent to a dung beetle named Ernest, who she claims lacked ambition. Ernest was the fourth Ernest. She does not see a pattern. Ethel once starred in a basement production of Gypsy, or so she claims, before the critics ran her out of town. She has never forgiven the press. She never will.

Up in the bathroom, perched on the mirror like a tiny gargoyle in evening dress, lives Sir Reginald Featherstonehaugh the Third. He insists on the full pronunciation: Fanshaw. Any deviation is met with a silence so cold it could frost a window in July. Reggie is a cellar spider with legs so long and elegant he looks like he's wearing Victorian kid gloves, the kind that button at the wrist. He fancies himself a minor aristocracy, exiled from a grand English manor after a scandal involving the lady of the house and a misplaced teacup. The details shift with each retelling, which is how you know it's a proper scandal. He spends his days vibrating his web in mournful tremolos, sighing about "the old estate" and complaining that American flies lack proper seasoning. Once, when I dropped a pill, he lowered himself on a silken thread like a chandelier butler and deposited it gently on the sink. "One does what one must," he muttered, then retreated to polish his already spotless fangs. I believe, in his quiet way, he considers this the highest form of noblesse oblige.

In the living room, behind the bookshelf crammed with dog eared paperbacks, hides Dolores Thudbury. Dolores is a bold jumping spider, glossy black with iridescent chevrons that flash like sequins on a ringmaster's coat. She was, in a former life, a circus performer in a traveling flea circus. She walked the high wire, leapt through flaming hoops the size of dimes, and once caught a fruit fly mid-flight in front of a paying crowd of one bored child and his suspicious grandmother. Retired now, she patrols the shelves like a tiny precinct captain, pouncing on silverfish with a bureaucratic precision that suggests she keeps files on them somewhere. If a book falls, she glares at me as if I've violated some ancient ordinance she personally drafted. I have learned not to shelve anything without her tacit approval.

Out on the sun porch, in a web strung between two dying succulents, lounges Hank "The Tank" McCrumb. Hank is a fat, satisfied cobweb spider who looks like he's wearing a permanent beer belly made of dust. He's a hoarder. His web is less a trap and more a junkyard: bits of leaf, dead ants, a single sequin I lost in 2019, and what might be half a Cheeto. Hank claims he was a prospector in the great Dust Bowl spider rush of '36, panning for crumbs in the cracks of Oklahoma farmhouses. He still talks about striking it rich one day when he finally catches "the big one," a housefly carrying a french fry. He knows it's out there. He can feel it. At night, he strums his web like a washtub bass and sings old hobo songs in a gravelly baritone that sounds like Tom Waits if Tom Waits were the size of a lentil.

Finally, tucked in the corner of the bedroom ceiling, where the paint peels like old love letters, resides Madame Esmeralda Velvetlegs. Esme is a stealth spider, small and dark and mysterious, the kind that appears and vanishes like a magician's assistant who got tired of the magician. She tells fortunes. Not with cards, but by reading the vibrations in her web, the way old women once read tea leaves. She predicted I'd burn toast on Tuesday (accurate), that a package would arrive late (also accurate), and that I'd find a twenty-dollar bill in an old coat pocket (still waiting, Esme). She claims centuries of Silk Road wanderers in her lineage, and she speaks with a thick, theatrical accent that somehow works even without a voice. When the moon is full, she lowers herself on a single thread, dangles in front of my face while I'm trying to sleep, and whispers cryptic advice like "Beware the moth with delusions of grandeur." I have never once known what to do with this information. I suspect that is the point.

These are my roommates, my tiny divas and dreamers, spinning their small operas in the corners of my world. I never squash them. How could I? They have names. They have stories. And every night, when the house settles into quiet, I swear I can hear Ethel warming up, Reggie sighing, Dolores drilling her silverfish dossiers, Hank humming, and Esme murmuring prophecies to the dark. It's the best dinner theater in the world, and the cover charge is just one careless fly.

Sometimes, when visitors come over, they ask why I never spray the corners. They say the house looks old, a little wild, like something is always just slightly alive behind the walls.

I tell them it's ventilation. Or ecology. Or that spiders eat the mosquitoes.

I don't tell them the truth.

The truth is that a house without witnesses feels abandoned. A house without small lives ticking away in the margins starts to sound too big, too hollow, like a church after the congregation has gone home. The spiders keep the place inhabited. They keep the air threaded with intention.

At night, when the refrigerator kicks off, and the pipes stop muttering, and even the dogs have settled into their slow submarine breathing, there's still movement. Still work being done. Still somebody awake. A tremor in the web. A soft skitter across plaster. A thread pulled tight. Proof that the world hasn't gone empty.

My mornings follow a route as fixed as any mail carrier's. Kitchen first, where I check Ethel's web for structural improvements and overnight catches. She's always adding, always expanding, her sticky palace growing by a thread or two each night. Then the bathroom, where Reggie receives me with the dignified tolerance of a butler who did not request visitors. A nod. A faint vibration. The audience concluded. Through the living room, where Dolores tracks my movements from the spine of a thick paperback, her eight eyes clocking me like security cameras with opinions. Out to the sun porch, where Hank's web catches the first light like a stained-glass window made of lint and ambition. And finally, though I never see her in the morning, I pause at the bedroom ceiling and note that Esme's web has been freshly adjusted. Tighter on the left. Looser on the right. A change in the forecast, perhaps. Or a whim. With Esme, these are frequently the same thing.

I know their schedules. Ethel rehearses between two and four in the morning. Reggie takes his constitutional vibration at precisely half past ten. Dolores runs patrol at dawn and dusk, bookending the day with purpose. Hank naps from breakfast through lunch, which he calls "conserving resources," and comes alive at twilight when the porch gnats begin their evening commute. Esme keeps no schedule at all, or keeps one so complex it merely appears like chaos, which is exactly how she'd want it.

They know my schedule too. They know when I'm cooking by the steam that rises. They know when I'm reading by the stillness. They know when I've had a bad day because I walk faster and touch nothing, and they know when I've had a good one because I hum, and Ethel hums back, and for a moment the kitchen sounds like a duet between a human and an orb-weaver, which is not a thing that should work, but does.

We have an understanding, the six of us. I provide the house. They provide the corners. I don't spray. They don't bite. I pretend they are ordinary spiders, and they pretend I am an ordinary landlord, and we all get along beautifully in the lie.

It was, by any measure, a perfect arrangement.

It was about to become a considerably less perfect one.

CHAPTER

TWO

THE ARRIVAL

I found her on a Tuesday, which Esme had already declared a day of minor significance and moderate peril.

She was dangling from the bathroom faucet on a single thread of silk so fine it looked like a crack in the air. Impossibly small. Barely more than a speck with legs. She turned slowly in the updraft from the drain, rotating like a tiny ballerina in a music box that had been wound by someone with very small fingers and very large hopes.

I leaned in. She leaned in. We regarded each other with the mutual curiosity of two creatures who had not expected company at the sink.

"Hello," I said, because I am the sort of person who talks to spiders, which you already know, or you would not still be reading this.

She waved one leg. Whether this was a greeting, a warning, or simply the result of air currents, I chose to interpret it as a greeting, because that was the more interesting option, and I was having a dull morning.

I named her Midge.

Midge was so small she could have ridden comfortably on a sesame seed and still had room for luggage. Her legs were translucent, the pale gold of watered-down honey, and her body was a single dark dot, like a period at the end of a very short sentence. She had no web to speak of, no territory, no apparent skills beyond the ability to dangle and look plaintive, which, to be fair, she did exceptionally well.

I told Reggie about her.

Reggie received the news the way he receives all news: with a long silence, a single vibration of his web that somehow conveyed both acknowledgment and disapproval, and a quiet remark about how standards had declined measurably since the previous century.

"One does not simply take in strays," he said, or seemed to say, adjusting a thread with the fussy precision of a man straightening a painting that was already straight.

"She's very small," I offered.

"That," said Reggie, "is hardly a qualification."

Ethel, on the other hand, was thrilled. She spotted Midge the same evening, when Midge had drifted on her thread from the bathroom faucet to the hallway ceiling, a journey of approximately eight feet that had taken her most of the afternoon and left her visibly winded.

"Look at her!" Ethel announced to no one and everyone. "Look at those legs! That posture! That poise!" Ethel has never met a small creature she could not immediately envision on a stage. She once tried to audition a confused moth who had wandered into her web, and was genuinely offended when it flew away. "She's got something," Ethel declared, and began humming what sounded like an overture.

Midge dangled from the hallway ceiling and did not respond to any of this, which Ethel interpreted as mysterious allure.

Dolores spotted Midge during her evening patrol and stopped so abruptly that her back four legs nearly overtook her front four, a phenomenon I have come to think of as the Dolores Pile-Up, and one that occurs whenever she encounters something she hasn't already catalogued. She circled Midge twice, evaluated her from seven of her eight eyes (the eighth being reserved for emergencies), and filed her, I can only assume, under "P" for "Pending" or possibly "T" for "Tolerable, Barely."

"Unregistered," Dolores muttered and moved on. In Dolores's world, this is neither acceptance nor rejection. It is bureaucratic limbo, which is where most things live until Dolores decides otherwise.

Hank did not notice Midge at all, because Hank does not notice things that are not food, not junk, and not directly in his web. Hank's awareness extends approximately three inches in every direction from his body, forming a sphere of attention so small and so devoted to personal comfort that it amounts to a kind of genius. He was asleep when Midge drifted past the porch doorway. He was still asleep when she drifted back. He would remain unaware of Midge's existence for another full day, at which point he would claim to have known about her all along and to have been "keeping an eye on the situation," which was a lie so transparent even his web could see through it.

Esme, of course, said nothing. She merely adjusted her web. Tighter on the left. Tighter still on the right. Both sides pulled inward, as if the web itself were holding its breath.

I should have paid more attention to this.

Esme's web adjustments, I have learned, are roughly as reliable as a barometer and considerably more specific. A loose web means calm. A tight web means weather. A web adjusted on both sides simultaneously means something is coming that

Esme considers noteworthy, and Esme does not find many things noteworthy. She once slept through a thunderstorm that knocked out the power for six hours. She barely stirred when a squirrel fell down the chimney and ran screaming through the living room while Dolores organized an emergency response and Ethel composed a ballad about the invasion in real time.

Both sides of the web. Pulled tight. Holding.

But I didn't notice, because I was busy watching Midge figure out how to climb a wall, which she did with the slow, wobbling determination of a toddler ascending a staircase built for adults. Two steps up. One step sideways. One step that seemed to go in no direction at all but somehow still counted as progress. She reached the corner where the wall meets the ceiling, settled into the angle like a comma in a long sentence, and went to sleep.

One more spider. Just one. One more tiny witness in the margins of the house.

I thought: how much trouble could one small spider be?

This, I believe, is what is known as dramatic irony. Or possibly hubris. Or possibly just the particular foolishness of a person who has lived with Ethel Merman for two years and still believes that anything in this house happens in small, manageable quantities.

Midge slept through the night. Reggie maintained his disapproval. Ethel planned an audition. Dolores updated her files. Hank snored. Esme held her web tight.

And in the dark, quiet spaces between the walls, where plaster meets timber and dust meets silk and the house keeps its oldest secrets, something was already happening.

Something small.

Something busy.

Something with approximately thirty two hundred legs and absolutely no intention of knocking first.

THREE

THE FLOOD

Wednesday morning began the way all catastrophes begin: with coffee.

I shuffled to the kitchen in my slippers, which is to say I shuffled approximately four steps before I walked through the first web. It caught me across the face like a veil I hadn't ordered, and I did the dance that all humans do when they walk through a web, which is a kind of full-body shudder combined with frantic hand-waving that communicates nothing useful to anyone and accomplishes even less.

I wiped my face. I took another step. I walked through a second web.

This was unusual. Ethel's web was in its customary location under the cabinet, and she did not generally expand into the hallway. Reggie would never build so low. Dolores didn't build at all; she was a jumper and considered webs to be, at best, a primitive technology. These webs were new. They were small. And they were everywhere.

I turned on the kitchen light.

The ceiling moved.

I don't mean the ceiling moved the way ceilings sometimes seem to move when you stand up too fast, or when the light catches a cobweb just so. I mean, the ceiling was in active, visible, undeniable motion. Hundreds of tiny bodies, each one barely larger than a grain of sand, scuttling and spinning and dangling and climbing and doing all the things that baby spiders do when they have just arrived in a world full of corners and possibilities and absolutely no supervision.

They were on the counters. They were on the cabinets. They were on the windowsill, the stove, the refrigerator handle, the fruit bowl (where three of them appeared to be attempting to summit a banana), and the toaster, from which a thin strand of silk rose like a flag planted on a conquered territory. They were on my coffee mug, which I had left on the counter the night before, and which now resembled a tiny apartment building with at least twenty occupants and no elevator.

I stood in the doorway and stared.

Ethel was already awake. Ethel was, in fact, wider awake than I had ever seen her. She sat at the center of her web with the electric energy of a woman who has just been handed a chorus line of fifty and told to make magic by curtain time. Her legs were moving in all directions, plucking threads, adjusting tensions, expanding borders. Her web had doubled in size overnight. She looked at me, and I swear, I swear on every tattered paperback in the living room, she winked.

I checked the bathroom next. The mirror was freckled with tiny dots that had not been there the night before. Reggie sat at the apex of his web, rigid as a flagpole, radiating a silence so total and so offended it could have curdled milk. Below him, a cluster of baby spiders had gathered on the soap dish and were, by all appearances, attempting to eat the soap.

"This," Reggie said, in the way that Reggie says things, which is to say he vibrated his web in a frequency I have come to associate with deep constitutional crisis, "this is entirely unacceptable."

The living room was worse. Or better, depending on your tolerance for chaos. The bookshelf had been colonized from top to bottom. Every gap between every book now contained a web, and every web contained a spider, and several of the spiders were making experimental jumps from shelf to shelf with the fearless incompetence of small creatures who have not yet learned that gravity has opinions. Dolores stood on the spine of a particularly thick dictionary, her body rigid, her chevrons flashing, surveying the invasion with the expression of a general who has arrived at the battlefield to find that the battlefield has also arrived at her.

The sun porch was a masterpiece of disaster. Hank's web, already a museum of accumulated debris, had become the center of a sprawling suburb of smaller webs that radiated outward like the spokes of a wheel, if the wheel had been designed by a committee of very ambitious but structurally illiterate baby spiders. Several of the babies had already taken up residence in Hank's collection, and one of them appeared to be sitting on the sequin with the territorial confidence of a creature who had found its throne.

Hank was asleep.

Of course he was.

I returned to the bedroom. Esme's web was exactly as it had been the night before. Tight on the left. Tight on the right. She sat at its center, perfectly still, perfectly calm, radiating the smug serenity of someone who had predicted the flood and packed accordingly.

"You knew," I said.

Esme said nothing, because Esme never says anything when she's right, which is her most infuriating quality and also, if I am being honest, her most impressive one. She merely adjusted a single thread. Looser now. Relaxed.

The storm had arrived. No sense holding the web tight anymore.

I went back to the kitchen. I made my coffee. I sat at the table. A baby spider descended from the light fixture on a thread of silk and landed on my wrist. It sat there, weightless and bewildered, like a tourist who had just gotten off at the wrong stop and was trying to figure out the map.

I looked at it. It looked at me. All eight eyes, each one a tiny black bead no bigger than the point of a pin.

"Right," I said. "Okay."

The spider on my wrist waved one leg, and from the ceiling, from the walls, from every corner and crevice and crack in the plaster, four hundred of its siblings waved back, and the house, which had been quietly extraordinary for two years, became something else entirely.

Something louder. Something stickier. Something that would require, I suspected, a great deal more coffee.

INTERLUDE
DOLORES THUDBURY

INCIDENT REPORT NO. 00347

Filed by: Dolores Thudbury, Chief of Patrol and
Domestic Surveillance
Date: Wednesday, the day everything went sideways
Location: All of it. Every single corner. The whole house.
Classification: Unprecedented

SUMMARY OF EVENTS:

At approximately 0547 hours, this officer completed her standard dawn patrol of Sector 3 (Living Room) and noted no irregularities. By 0612 hours, this officer had noted four hundred and seventeen irregularities, all of them very small and none of them authorized.

DESCRIPTION OF IRREGULARITIES:

Small. Numerous. Leggy.

RESPONSE:

This officer attempted to conduct a census. This officer was unable to conduct a census because the subjects would not stop moving. This officer attempted to organize the subjects into orderly rows. This officer was unsuccessful. This officer attempted to assign identification numbers. This officer ran out of numbers.

DAMAGE ASSESSMENT:

Sector 1 (Kitchen): Webs in every cabinet. Subjects observed on banana (three), toaster (seven), coffee mug (twenty, estimated), and inside sugar bowl (number unknown, sugar bowl now classified as compromised).

Sector 2 (Bathroom): Soap dish occupation confirmed. Mirror visibility reduced by approximately forty percent. Sir Reginald's formal complaint acknowledged and filed.

Sector 3 (Living Room): Full colonization of bookshelf. The structural integrity of the existing filing system is threatened. Subjects observed jumping between volumes with no regard for the Dewey Decimal System or any other system.

Sector 4 (Sun Porch): Lost cause. Recommend quarantine.

Sector 5 (Bedroom): Madame Esmeralda reports no concerns. Madame Esmeralda never reports concerns. This officer finds Madame Esmeralda's calm suspicious.

RECOMMENDATIONS:

This officer recommends the immediate establishment of a registration process, a meal distribution schedule, a curfew, and possibly a very small school.

This officer further recommends that Hank "The Tank" McCrumb be formally notified that his sector is now a suburb. Request for notification pending, as Hank "The Tank" McCrumb is asleep.

STATUS: Ongoing.

ADDENDUM: This officer would like it noted, for the record, that she predicted nothing, assumed nothing, and was in no way prepared for this. This officer would also like it noted that she intends to handle it anyway.

That is what officers do.

CHAPTER

FOUR

THE FOSTERING

By Thursday, it became clear that four hundred baby spiders could not simply wander the house like tourists at a museum with no docent and no closing time. Someone had to take charge. Several someones thought they already had.

The Fostering, as I came to call it, was not a meeting. Spiders do not hold meetings. What spiders do is occupy space with such intensity and specificity that territories emerge, borders form, and custody arrangements materialize out of thin air and silk, which in this house amounts to the same thing.

Ethel moved first, because Ethel always moves first. By Wednesday evening, she had expanded her web to three times its original size, annexing the entire underside of the kitchen cabinet and most of the counter's edge. Into this sticky empire she gathered every baby spider within reach, which turned out to be about sixty, and began sorting them with the brisk efficiency of a casting director on the first day of auditions.

"You," she said, pointing one leg at a cluster of wide eyed

spiderlings huddled near the toaster. "Front row. You, you, and you, second row. You in the back, stop eating your sister. Everyone else, find a spot and look alive, because we have a lot of work to do and I haven't had this many performers since the summer of '58, which was a magnificent season and also a complete disaster, and we are not going to talk about what happened with the centipede."

Nobody asked about the centipede. This is a rule in Ethel's web that predates the babies and will outlast them.

Reggie's approach was, predictably, the opposite. He did not recruit. He did not expand. He tightened his borders and issued, through a series of precise web vibrations, what I can only describe as an immigration policy. Applicants would be considered on a case by case basis. References were preferred. Prior experience in civilized behavior was required. Loud noises, sudden movements, and any form of what Reggie called "gallivanting" would result in immediate and permanent expulsion.

Four baby spiders met his criteria. He accepted them with the air of a headmaster admitting charity scholars to an institution that preferred not to need them. They sat in a neat row at the edge of his web, very still, very quiet, and very much aware that one wrong vibration would send them back to the general population.

One of these four was a tiny cellar spider, all legs and no confidence, who seemed to have been born already apologizing. Reggie looked at this one for a long time. The baby looked back with an expression that, in a creature with fewer eyes, would have been called hopeful.

"Adequate," Reggie pronounced, which, in the language of Sir Reginald Featherstonehaugh the Third, is the highest compliment available to a newcomer and should be received with gratitude and no visible emotion.

Dolores, true to form, organized a draft.

She did this by establishing a processing station on the third shelf of the bookcase, between a collection of mystery novels and a water-stained atlas that had been there so long it had become furniture. Every baby spider that wandered into the living room was intercepted, evaluated, and assigned a designation. Dolores had categories. Dolores always has categories.

Category A: Physically fit, alert, responsive to instruction. Suitable for patrol training.

Category B: Average fitness, moderate alertness, tendency to wander. Suitable for support roles.

Category C: Below average in all respects. Suitable for filing.

Category D: Ate the assessment form.

Dolores took about thirty, mostly A's and B's, with a handful of C's she claimed were "project cases" and one D she kept an eye on for reasons she declined to share. She arranged them in rows on the shelf, conducted a headcount, conducted another headcount because three of them had moved, conducted a third headcount because one of the ones she'd counted was actually a piece of lint, and then began patrol orientation, which consisted of marching them back and forth along the shelf edge while she supervised from the dictionary.

Hank, when he finally woke up, handled the situation the way Hank handles all situations: by not handling it.

"Kids!" he said, as if discovering them for the first time, despite the fact that at least twenty of them had been living in his web since before dawn. "Well, what do you know. Company." He looked around at the small bodies scattered across his web, tangled in his collection, perched on his Cheeto, and shrugged, which, for Hank, involves all eight legs, takes about four seconds, and looks like a very slow wave.

"Make yourselves at home," he told them. "Touch the sequin, and there'll be trouble."

Nobody touched the sequin. Several touched everything else. Hank watched them with the benign indifference of a man whose standards could not get any lower and who was perfectly comfortable with this fact.

Esme accepted three.

Three. Out of four hundred.

She descended from the bedroom ceiling on a single thread, surveyed the hallway traffic of wandering spiderlings with the unhurried gaze of someone selecting fruit at a market, and tapped three of them. Just a tap. One light touch of one leg on each small body. Then she climbed back up, and the three followed, silent, as if they had been waiting for exactly this and nothing else.

The rest of the babies, the ones not claimed by any of the five tenants, did what unclaimed baby spiders do. They scattered. They explored. They built webs in places no web had any business being: inside shoes, across doorframes, between the salt and pepper shakers, under the dog's water bowl, and in one case, stretched across the bathroom doorway at exactly nose height, which I discovered at six in the morning in the dark, and which I would like to say I handled with dignity, but cannot.

By Friday, the house had been partitioned into five distinct child-rearing operations, each reflecting the philosophy, personality, and particular neuroses of its founder, and none of them agreeing with any of the others about anything, ever, at all.

It was, I realized, watching Ethel audition her sixty while Reggie lectured his four while Dolores drilled her thirty while Hank napped among his twenty while Esme whispered to her three, exactly like every neighborhood I have ever lived in, except smaller and stickier and with more legs per capita.

And the unclaimed ones, the wanderers, the ones nobody picked, they kept drifting through the hallways like small ghosts, building their crooked little webs in forgotten places, getting by.

Somebody, I thought, ought to check on those ones.

But I had just walked through another web, and it was only Friday, and already the coffee was not strong enough.

CHAPTER

FIVE

THE EDUCATION

The trouble with raising someone, even if that someone is the size of a poppy seed and has eight legs, is that you inevitably try to make them into a version of yourself. This is true of humans, and it is true, I can now confirm, of spiders. Possibly more so. Humans at least have the decency to pretend they're encouraging independence. Spiders skip the pretense entirely and get straight to the curriculum.

Ethel's academy opened on Saturday.

She had, overnight, restructured her web into something that resembled a theater in the round, if the round were slightly oval, made of silk, and suspended beneath a kitchen cabinet that smelled of old coffee. At the center sat Ethel. Around her, arranged in concentric semicircles like a tiny amphitheater, sat her sixty students, most of whom were awake, some of whom were paying attention, and one of whom was trying to eat the spider next to it.

"Stop that," Ethel said, in the same tone she once used to address a beetle she'd called a "no talent hack". The cannibal stopped. Ethel had that effect.

22

The first lesson was projection. Not web projection. Voice projection. Ethel believed, with the unshakeable conviction of a six-time divorcee who had never once blamed herself for anything, that every spider had a voice, and that every voice deserved to be heard, preferably at a volume that could reach the back of the room, and the room next to it, and possibly the neighbors.

"From the thorax!" she bellowed. "Not the spinnerets! The thorax! You're singing, not spinning! There's a difference, and it matters!"

Sixty baby spiders attempted to sing. The result was a sound I can only compare to a very small radiator trying to harmonize with a tuning fork that had been dropped in honey. It was not music. It was not even noise in any organized sense. It was the sound of pure, unfiltered effort, coming from creatures who had been alive for less than a week and were already being asked to belt it to the cheap seats.

Ethel was delighted.

"Gorgeous!" she cried. "Terrible, but gorgeous! Again! Louder! And you, third row, what's your name?"

The spider in the third row, a compact little orb weaver with markings that looked like a tiny bow tie, vibrated uncertainly.

"Wodehouse," Ethel decided, because Ethel names things the way she does everything else: immediately, confidently, and without consulting anyone. "You've got timing. I don't know what you've got timing for yet, but you've got it. Stay after class."

Wodehouse stayed after class. Wodehouse would always stay after class, not because he was the most talented but because he was the most willing, and because he had a quality that Ethel recognized instantly, the ability to be slightly wrong in the most perfectly pleasant way, so that the wrongness itself became a kind of charm.

Three rows back, another baby spider sat apart from the group. This one was dark and still and smaller than the others, with a stillness that wasn't shy but deliberate, like a portrait that had decided to observe the museum rather than the other way around. It did not attempt to sing. It did not attempt anything. It simply sat and watched with a focused intensity that made the spiders on either side of it scoot a little farther away without knowing why.

Ethel named this one Gorey.

Gorey did not acknowledge the name. Gorey did not acknowledge anything. Gorey simply existed with the quiet, unsettling certainty of a creature who had arrived in the world already knowing something the rest of them hadn't figured out yet. Over the coming days, Gorey would be found in increasingly improbable locations: on the spine of a book about Victorian funerary customs, inside an empty inkwell, hanging motionless from the bathroom ceiling directly above where Reggie slept, staring down at him with all eight eyes like a very small audit.

Reggie's finishing school, by contrast, ran on silence and standards.

His four pupils sat in a perfect line at the edge of his web, and Reggie walked the line like an inspector reviewing troops, except the troops were the size of sesame seeds and the inspector was the size of a small paper clip with delusions of grandeur.

"Posture," he said to the first. The first straightened.

"Posture," he said to the second. The second was already straight. Reggie nodded. This was approval.

"Posture," he said to the third. The third wobbled. Reggie sighed. The sigh lasted approximately three seconds, which in

Reggie's emotional vocabulary represents a crisis of faith in the younger generation.

The fourth, the small cellar spider who had been born apologizing, sat so straight and so still that it appeared to have stopped breathing, which, in spiders, is not as alarming as it sounds but was still, in this context, a bit much.

"Adequate," Reggie told it. The baby relaxed by approximately one degree. This was progress.

Reggie's curriculum covered web etiquette (never vibrate louder than necessary), dining protocol (always approach a caught fly from the proper angle), personal grooming (fangs polished twice daily, no exceptions), and conversation (topics restricted to weather, architecture, and the decline of modern fly quality). He did not teach singing, dancing, or any art form that required enthusiasm. Enthusiasm, in Reggie's view, was a character flaw best left to Americans and orb-weavers, and he saw no reason to encourage it.

He did, however, teach one thing that none of the other adults taught: stillness. How to sit on a web and wait. How to let the world come to you. How to be quiet, not because you had nothing to say but because you had decided that saying it was beneath you. His four students learned this well. Perhaps too well. Within a week, the bathroom had become the quietest room in the house, which, given that it contained a mirror, a faucet, and four tiny aristocrats in-training, was both impressive and slightly eerie.

Dolores's boot camp was the loudest operation in the living room, which was saying something, given that Ethel's kitchen rehearsals could be heard through the wall.

Dolores did not teach art. Dolores did not teach etiquette. Dolores taught competence.

Morning drills began at dawn. The baby spiders lined up on the shelf edge and practiced jumps. Not pretty jumps. Not artistic jumps. Functional jumps. Point A to Point B. No wasted motion. No showing off. Dolores had constructed an obstacle course from a paperclip, a rubber band, and what appeared to be a straightened staple, and every morning her recruits ran it while she watched from the dictionary, her iridescent chevrons catching the early light like medals on a general who had earned every single one of them.

Among her thirty, one stood out. A bold little jumping spider with oversized front legs and a habit of landing on targets that hadn't been assigned to her. She jumped farther than the others, landed harder than the others, and, when corrected, looked at Dolores with an expression that was not defiance exactly, but something close to it. Something that said: I heard you. I understood you. I am going to do it my way regardless.

Dolores named her Zora.

Zora did not stay in formation. Zora did not follow the route. Zora built her own web on the windowsill, the most sun exposed, most dangerous, most visible spot in the living room, and sat in it with the absolute confidence of a creature who had decided that if the world was going to come for her, it could come in full daylight where she could see it.

Dolores disapproved. Dolores respected it. These two things lived comfortably side by side in Dolores's personality, the way a filing cabinet can hold both commendations and complaints in the same drawer.

Another of Dolores's recruits, a twitchy little spider who jumped at everything, including his own shadow and occasionally his own legs, she named Thurber. Thurber bumped into things. Thurber got tangled in his own silk. Thurber once jumped at a piece of dust, missed, and landed in Hank's web, where he sat stunned and trembling until Dolores sent a retrieval team. Despite all this, or perhaps because of all this,

Thurber never quit. He showed up every morning, slightly rumpled, slightly confused, and ready to try again. Dolores moved him from combat training to filing duty, where his nervous energy translated into a furious organizational zeal that made him, against all odds, the most productive clerk in the outfit.

Hank's educational philosophy could be summarized in four words: figure it out, kid.

His twenty-odd charges roamed the sun porch web in a state of cheerful anarchy. They ate what they found. They built where they wanted. They fought, played, slept, and woke in no particular order and on no particular schedule. Several of them had burrowed into Hank's collection and now lived among the dead ants and leaf fragments like tiny settlers in a junkyard frontier town.

Hank presided over this chaos from his spot at the center of the web, offering occasional wisdom in the form of short, gruff observations that may or may not have been meant as advice.

"See that gnat? That's dinner."

"Don't eat things bigger than your head."

"Your brother's not food. Well. Not yet."

One of Hank's crew was a stocky little cobweb spider who had, within hours of arrival, begun collecting things. A crumb. A flake of paint. A fragment of a leaf so small it was barely a concept. This spider arranged its treasures in a careful line at the edge of the web and guarded them with a fierceness that was wildly disproportionate to their value, which was zero.

Hank looked at this spider. The spider looked at Hank. They understood each other perfectly.

"That one's Saki," Hank said, though I'm not sure who he was talking to. Possibly himself. Possibly the sequin.

Saki was small and vicious and perfectly composed, and she

would, in the weeks to come, build the most impressive personal collection on the porch, a miniature empire of lint and found objects that she defended with a ferocity that suggested she had been born knowing that the world takes things from you if you let it, and she had no intention of letting it.

Esme's three sat on the bedroom ceiling in a small circle, doing something I could not identify.

They were not spinning. They were not jumping. They were not eating. They were sitting in a triangle, perfectly still, while Esme sat above them and occasionally touched a thread that connected their positions, sending a vibration through the web that they seemed to absorb like a lesson delivered in a language I did not speak.

One of them kept trying to eat the web. Esme watched this one with particular attention and said, to no one in particular, "This one has the gift."

Nobody knew what the gift was. The baby spider chewed on the silk and looked vacant. Esme looked certain.

The third of Esme's students was different from the other two. This one did not sit still. It wandered to the edge of the web, hung over the side, and stared down at the floor below with a concentration so intense it seemed to be trying to see through the floorboards to whatever lay beneath.

I did not name this one. Esme did not name this one. It named itself, or rather, it simply became what it was: the one who looked at things no one else was looking at, the one who sat at edges, the one who was always almost falling but never quite did.

I thought of it as Lear. But only to myself.

And then there were the others. The unclaimed. The ones who belonged to no academy, no finishing school, no boot camp, no commune, no mystical circle. They drifted through the house in twos and threes, building webs in the spaces between territories, eating what they could find, learning what they could steal from the edges of someone else's lesson. Some of them were bold. Some of them were barely there. One of them, a spider so pale it was almost transparent, had built a web in the shadow behind the refrigerator where no light reached and no one looked, and it sat there, day after day, doing nothing remarkable, catching what drifted in, existing.

I checked on that one. I checked on it every morning.

It never moved. It never grew. It never built anything impressive, caught anything memorable, or did a single thing that any of the other four hundred would notice or remember.

But it was there. Every morning. Still there. Still spinning. Still holding on.

Every house needs a few of those, too.

INTERLUDE
HANK "THE TANK" MCCRUMB

HANK'S LEDGER

INVENTORY OF GOODS, ASSETS, AND MISCELLANEOUS ITEMS

Proprietor: Hank "The Tank" McCrumb

Location: The Porch (all of it, I was here first)

One (1) sequin, silver, origin unknown, possibly from a lady's evening garment or possibly from the ceiling. Do not touch. This means you.

One (1) half a Cheeto, vintage, well-aged, no longer orange but a distinguished amber. Sentimental value. Also, possibly still edible. Have not tested this. Will not test this. It is not about the eating. It is about the having.

Three (3) dead ants, assorted sizes. Decorative.

One (1) fragment of a leaf, brown, curled at the edges like a tiny scroll. Could contain a message. Have not unrolled it. Might be important. Might be nothing. That's the thrill.

Seven (7) pieces of dust are significant. Not regular dust. Good dust. The kind that settles with purpose.

One (1) thing that might be a crumb or might be a very small rock. Classification pending. Have licked it. Inconclusive.

Fourteen (14) baby spiders are resident. Or sixteen. They move around. Hard to count. Do not subtract any of them without written permission, which I do not know how to write, so effectively, do not subtract any of them.

One (1) baby spider (Saki), currently operating a secondary collection within the borders of this collection, which I am allowing because she has good taste and because she bit me when I suggested otherwise.

LOSSES THIS WEEK:

One (1) gnat wing, stolen. Suspect: unknown baby spider, small, fast, no remorse.

One (1) strand of web, repurposed without authorization by a baby spider who used it to build what can only be described as a hammock. I am not angry. I am impressed. But I am also angry.

GAINS THIS WEEK:

One (1) flake of something gold. Found on the windowsill. It could be paint. It could be treasure. I'm treating it as treasure until proven otherwise.

MARKET OBSERVATIONS:

Demand for food is up. The supply of food is down. Somebody ate all the gnats. I have my suspicions, but I am not naming names because I am a professional.

The economy is in what I would call "a rough patch." I am calling it an opportunity. When things are scarce, things have value. When things have value, the man with the Cheeto is king.

CLOSING REMARKS:

Everybody wants something. Nobody's got enough. Same as it ever was.

Hank "The Tank" McCrumb

Proprietor, Prospector, and Patient Man

CHAPTER

SIX

THE ECONOMY

The flies ran out on a Monday.

Not all at once. Flies do not disappear the way a light goes off. They disappear the way a river dries: slowly, then faster, then you're standing on cracked mud, wondering where the water went and when, exactly, you should have started worrying.

The first week after the flood, there were plenty. A house with dogs and a kitchen and a back door that doesn't close properly has always had a reliable supply of small, stupid flying things that blunder in and never blunder out. Ethel caught her share. Reggie caught his. Dolores hunted with precision. Hank caught whatever landed in his web by accident, which was his entire business model and had served him well for years. Even the babies, clumsy as they were, managed to snag the occasional gnat.

But four hundred extra mouths changed the math.

By the second week, the gnats were sparse. By the third, the fruit flies had all but vanished. The pantry moths, once so plentiful that I considered them a permanent feature of the kitchen, had dwindled to a handful of survivors who now flew in tight, nervous patterns near the ceiling, aware, in the dim way that moths are aware of anything, that the odds had shifted against them.

I noticed it first on Ethel's web. Her catches, normally a respectable three or four per day, had dropped to one. Then none. She sat at the center of her expanded empire, surrounded by sixty hungry students, and for the first time since I'd known her, she was quiet.

Ethel quiet is more alarming than Ethel loud.

The economy that emerged was neither planned nor fair, which is to say it was an economy.

Dolores organized it. Of course she did. Within hours of the first missed meal, she had established supply lines, rationing protocols, and a distribution system that routed whatever food was caught through a central processing point on the third shelf of the bookcase. Every catch was logged. Every portion was measured. Every spider in her jurisdiction received a fair share, which meant every spider in her jurisdiction received not quite enough, which is what fair means when there isn't enough to go around.

Ethel refused to participate in the rationing system.

"Rationing," she said, in a tone that suggested the word itself was a personal insult, "is for people without talent. My performers eat when they perform, and they perform when they eat, and if the system cannot accommodate art, then the system is broken, and I will not be a part of it."

What Ethel did instead was institute a cover charge. Attendance at her nightly shows, which had been free and open to any spider within earshot, now cost one gnat per seat. This was outrageous, given that gnats had become the scarcest commodity in the house. It was also effective. Spiders came. Spiders paid. Ethel's cast ate.

Reggie, who had only four mouths to feed and a web in the bathroom where the occasional drain fly still wandered in, was less affected than the others. He said nothing about this. He did not gloat. But his silence on the matter carried a particular quality: that of a man who has always believed that a smaller household is a more dignified household, and who is now being proven right and enjoying it in the most restrained way possible.

His four students ate sparingly, complained never, and maintained their posture throughout. Reggie considered this proof that good breeding triumphs over adversity. I considered it proof that hungry spiders don't fidget.

Hank opened the black market on a Wednesday.

I don't know when he planned it. I don't know how he planned it. Planning requires forethought, and Hank has always struck me as a creature for whom forethought is an optional accessory, like a hat. But somewhere between the food shortage and the rising desperation, Hank looked at his collection, looked at the hungry spiders drifting past his porch, and arrived at the most Hank realization possible: he had things, they wanted things, and want is the engine of commerce.

He started with the crumbs. Tiny fragments of food, so old and so dry they were more archaeology than nutrition, but food is food when you're hungry, and the bables were hungry. A piece of crumb costs one dead ant, delivered to Hank's web. A larger piece costs two. A truly premium crumb, the kind that might once have been bread or possibly a cracker, cost three dead ants and a piece of lint, because Hank liked lint and saw no reason not to diversify his portfolio.

Business was brisk.

Within days, Hank's web had transformed from a junkyard into a trading post. Spiders came from all over the house. Ethel's students traded captured gnats for crumbs. Dolores's recruits traded patrol hours for supplies. The unclaimed wanderers, the ones who belonged to nobody, traded whatever they could find: a bit of web, a dead mite, a small piece of nothing that Hank accepted anyway because Hank never turned down a deal and never turned away a customer.

Saki, Hank's most devoted student, ran a subsidiary operation from the corner of the web. She traded items from her personal collection at rates that were, even by Hank's flexible standards, extortionate. A flake of paint for two gnats. A fragment of dust for a fruit fly wing. She had the cold eye of a spider who understood supply and demand in her spinnerets and felt no particular need to be liked.

The only spider who did not participate in the economy was Esme.

Esme did not trade. Esme did not ration. Esme did not, as far as I could tell, worry about food at all. Her three students sat on the bedroom ceiling in their small triangle and seemed to subsist on vibrations and mystery, which is not a nutritional strategy I would recommend, but which appeared to be working.

When I checked on them, Esme's web was the same as always. Not tighter. Not looser. Perfectly calibrated. She looked at me the way she always did, which was the way a woman looks at someone who has just asked an obvious question and is about to receive a very unhelpful answer.

"The web provides," she said. Or seemed to say. Or vibrated in a frequency that my brain, desperate for meaning, translated into those words.

I left a fruit fly near the bedroom door that night. By morning, it was gone. Esme's web had not moved. The three babies sat in their triangle, well-fed and inscrutable.

The peak of the food crisis came at the end of the third week. Ethel's shows had gotten shorter because her cast was too tired to perform full sets. Dolores's recruits had slowed on patrol. Hank's crumb supply was running low, and the prices on the black market had climbed so high that only Saki could afford anything, which she could because she'd been hoarding since birth. Even Reggie's four had grown quieter than usual, which in Reggie's bathroom meant a silence so profound it felt geological.

I did something I am not proud of, although I am not ashamed of it either.

I left the kitchen window open.

Not all the way. Just a crack. Just enough to let the evening air in, and with it, the small parade of gnats and moths and midges and no-see-ums that gather at the edge of any lit window on a summer night, drawn by warmth and light and whatever dim impulse passes for hope in a creature with a two-day lifespan.

They came in. They flew to the light. They found the webs.

I did not watch what happened next. I went to the living room and read a book while, behind me, the kitchen filled with the soft sounds of an ecosystem rebalancing itself: the hum of wings, the pluck of silk, and the quiet, busy contentment of four hundred spiders who had just been delivered from famine by an open window and a landlord who had picked a side.

Ethel sang that night. Full voice. Three encores.

The economy stabilized. The black market continued, as black markets always do, but the desperation eased, and the prices came down, and the house settled into a new normal that was louder, messier, stickier than the old normal, but, in its own tangled way, functional.

I left the window cracked from then on.

It seemed like the least a landlord could do.

INTERLUDE
MADAME ESMERALDA VELVETLEGS

THE PROPHECIES OF MADAME ESMERALDA VELVETLEGS

Collected, with some difficulty, from vibrations in the bedroom web. Accuracy rating included where verifiable. Usefulness rating included where applicable, which is never.

"A great wind will carry small travelers to places they did not choose. This is not a tragedy. This is Tuesday."
(Accuracy: Unknown. Usefulness: None.)

"The one who hoards will find that what he keeps is less valuable than what he trades. Except for the sequin. The sequin is forever."
(Accuracy: Surprisingly high. Usefulness: Hank ignored it.)

"Something sticky approaches from the south. It brings change and also a mild inconvenience near the toaster."
(Accuracy: Confirmed. A baby spider built a web across the toast slot. Toast was delayed by twenty minutes.)

"Three will become many. Many will become few. Few will become enough. This is the arithmetic of corners."

(Accuracy: Pending. Usefulness: This is either profound or meaningless, which Esme considers the same thing.)

"Beware the moth with delusions of grandeur."

(Accuracy: Evergreen. There is always a moth with delusions of grandeur.)

"The singer will teach. The soldier will file. The gentleman will bend. The prospector will share. The seer will watch. The small one behind the refrigerator will remain."

(Accuracy: Under review. Several of these predictions seem to be about things that have not happened yet, which is either proof that Esme sees the future or proof that Esme makes vague enough statements that the future eventually catches up.)

"Someone will step on a web tomorrow. It will not be the end of the world. It will feel like the end of the world. These are different things."

(Accuracy: Confirmed. It was me. It was Ethel's. She rebuilt it by lunch and added a wing.)

"When the house is quietest, listen. What you hear is not silence. It is the sound of someone still working."

(Accuracy: Always.)

CHAPTER

SEVEN

THE TROUBLES

I should say, before I describe what happened next, that I do not blame anyone. Not Ethel, whose ambitions were theatrical and therefore boundless. Not Reggie, whose standards were impossible and therefore always being violated. Not Dolores, whose order was only as strong as the weakest recruit, and the weakest recruit had just gone AWOL. Not Hank, whose philosophy of benign neglect turned out to have a shelf life. Not Esme, who predicted everything and prevented nothing, which I suppose is the job description of a prophet, but is still deeply irritating when you're the one stepping into the consequences.

And not the babies. Especially not the babies. They were just doing what babies do, which is everything, all at once, with no plan, no caution, and no understanding that the world was not specifically designed for their convenience.

The Troubles began, as most troubles do, with a romance.

One of Reggie's students, the smallest and most fastidious of the four, a cellar spider so refined in its movements that it appeared to be dancing even when it was standing still, had

41

been making excursions. Quiet ones. Late at night. Down from the bathroom, through the hallway, past the kitchen, and out to the sun porch, where it sat at the very edge of Hank's web and looked in.

At what, I did not immediately understand. And then I did.

One of Hank's feral crew, a dusty, rumpled little cobweb spider with a smudge of something unidentifiable on its abdomen and the confident slouch of a creature who had never been told to sit up straight, had been looking back.

They met in the hallway. In a web that neither of them had built, strung between the baseboard and the leg of a small table, a web so delicate and so poorly constructed that it could not have been made by anyone with experience, which meant it had been made by someone with hope, which is a much more dangerous building material.

I found them there on a Thursday morning, sitting side by side in this crooked little web, perfectly still, perfectly content, and so obviously, flagrantly, impossibly mismatched that I understood immediately why it was going to be a problem.

Reggie found out by Friday.

The vibration that went through the bathroom web was not his usual mournful tremolo. It was not the dignified shudder of a spider encountering poor seasoning or American slang. It was the sharp, staccato pulse of genuine distress, the vibration equivalent of a man who has just discovered that his most promising student has been fraternizing with the lower orders and is not sure whether to be furious or ill and has settled on both.

"This," Reggie pronounced, from the height of his mirror, "will not stand."

It stood.

The two young spiders continued to meet in their hallway

web. Reggie forbade it. They ignored him. He vibrated disapproval at frequencies that could have etched glass. They were not glass. They were young, and they had found each other, and no amount of aristocratic dismay was going to change the geography of the hallway or the stubbornness of a cellar spider in love.

Hank, for his part, was unbothered.

"Kid wants to hang out in the hallway, kid hangs out in the hallway," he said, from deep within his web, where he was supervising nothing and comfortable with it. "Free country. Free porch. Free hallway. I didn't raise them to ask permission."

"You didn't raise them at all," I said.

"Exactly," said Hank, with the satisfaction of a man whose parenting philosophy had just been validated by its own absence.

Meanwhile, Ethel's household was fracturing along artistic lines.

The sixty had become, over the weeks, several factions. There were the singers, who had absorbed Ethel's lessons and could now produce a sound that, while not technically music, was at least recognizably intentional. There were the non-singers, who had been reassigned to set design and web construction and who resented the singers with the deep, abiding resentment of backstage crews everywhere. And there were Ethel's particular favourites, a small group of six or seven who had been given solo parts, special positions, and the lion's share of whatever food came in, which the rest of the sixty noticed and did not appreciate.

The mutiny, when it came, was silent. Spiders don't shout. They just leave.

One morning, a dozen of Ethel's non-singers packed up their silk and moved to the hallway, where they established an independent web collective that answered to nobody and performed nothing and existed solely as a rebuke to the concept of auditions. Ethel pretended not to notice. Ethel noticed everything. She simply expanded her remaining troupe's parts to fill the gaps and rehearsed twice as hard, because in Ethel's world, the show does not stop for defections, divorces, or acts of God, and she should know, having survived all three, most of them more than once.

Dolores lost Thurber.

Not lost in the permanent sense. Lost in the sense that Thurber, the twitchy, bumbling, perpetually startled spider who had been reassigned from combat to filing, had wandered out of the living room during a routine shelf patrol and ended up in Hank's web.

This was not, in itself, unusual. Spiders wander. Babies especially. What was unusual was that Thurber did not come back.

He was found three days later, sitting in a hammock he had woven between two dead ants in Hank's collection, eating a crumb of something ancient, and looking more relaxed than he had ever looked in his entire short life. He had stopped twitching. He had stopped jumping at his own shadow. He was, by all appearances, happy, in the way that only a creature who has finally found a place messy enough to match his insides can be happy.

Dolores filed a report. The report was four lines long. It read:

Subject: Thurber.

Status: AWOL.

Location: Sector 4 (Hank's web).

Recommendation: Let him stay.

That last line cost her something. I could tell by the way she wrote it, which is to say, I could tell by the way she sat on the dictionary afterward, very still, for a very long time, looking at nothing.

The sibling situation reached a peak on a Saturday. In Ethel's web, two of the larger babies had been competing for the same solo part in what Ethel was calling "the season finale," and the competition had escalated from artistic rivalry to something more primal and more eight-legged.

I walked into the kitchen to find one of them sitting on top of the other.

Not in a friendly way. Not in a playful way. In the way that spiders sit on other spiders when they have temporarily forgotten that the other spider is a sibling and not a snack.

"Coyote," I said.

Coyote looked up. Coyote had been named by Ethel in a moment of whimsy that I suspected was aimed at me, though she would never confirm this. Coyote was a round, enthusiastic little spider with more appetite than sense and a habit of treating every interaction as a potential meal. Coyote did not mean harm. Coyote simply had a very broad definition of "food" that occasionally included relatives.

"Coyote, we have talked about this. Put your brother down."

Coyote put his brother down. His brother, a slightly smaller spider named Lear (who had, without anyone's permission, migrated from Esme's ceiling to Ethel's web, driven by some internal gravity toward drama that even Esme couldn't contain), scrambled away and took up a position behind Ethel, where he vibrated with outrage and what I suspected was a monologue, silent but passionate, about injustice and ingratitude and the general decline of civilization, all delivered to an audience of none.

Lear was like that. Lear was always performing to the

storm, even when the storm was just his brother trying to eat him.

The sugar bowl incident happened on a Sunday.

I had been warned. Dolores's incident report from week one had classified the sugar bowl as "compromised." I had cleaned it out, or thought I had. I had not thought hard enough.

The sugar bowl was a nursery.

I discovered this when I opened the lid to sweeten my coffee and found, instead of sugar, approximately forty baby spiders sitting in a powdery white landscape like tiny mountaineers on a very sweet glacier. They looked up at me. I looked down at them. Nobody moved.

I closed the lid.

I drank my coffee black.

The webs across the doorways were the worst of it, because doorways are, in a house, what highways are in a country: the routes that everyone uses and nobody owns, and when someone builds a structure across one, everything slows down. I walked through an average of six webs per day. I developed a technique, a sort of slow-motion karate chop with one hand extended in front of my face, that cleared the path without destroying too much and made me look, I am certain, completely ridiculous to anyone who might have been watching, which, in this house, was everyone, because four hundred spiders have a collective total of three thousand two hundred eyes, and every single one of them was pointed at me.

The thought of the broom crossed my mind once.

Just once. On a Wednesday, after I had walked through the seventh web before noon and found a baby spider in my coffee cup and another one on my toothbrush and a third one rappelling down the inside of the lampshade like a tiny commando on a mission that had no clear objective and no extraction plan.

I thought: I could sweep them out. Gently. Carefully. Set the broom by the back door and let them disperse into the yard. Nobody gets hurt. The house gets a little breathing room. A little space. A little less silk in the sugar bowl.

I thought about it for exactly four seconds.

Then I heard Ethel start her evening rehearsal. And Reggie sighs. And Dolores marches her recruits along the shelf. And Hank hums. And somewhere in the bedroom, Esme adjusts a thread.

I put the thought away. I put it in the same place I keep all the thoughts I'm not proud of: somewhere behind the refrigerator, in the dark, where no one looks.

Where one small, pale spider was still sitting. Still spinning. Still there.

I drank my coffee black and let the house be what it was.

INTERLUDE
SIR REGINALD FEATHERSTONEHAUGH III

A LETTER TO THE MANAGEMENT

From the Desk of Sir Reginald Featherstonehaugh III
  The Bathroom Mirror, Upper Left Quadrant
  (The Proper Quadrant)
  To: The Management (i.e., the Large One Who Controls
  the Faucets)

Dear Sir or Madam,

I write to you not in anger, for anger is the province of those who have lost command of themselves, and I have not, but in a state of measured and entirely justified concern regarding the current conditions in what was, until very recently, a well-ordered household.

I shall be specific, as specificity is the hallmark of a civilized complaint, and I am, if nothing else, civilized.

Item the First: The noise. It was tolerable when it originated solely from the kitchen, where a certain theatrical personage has always conducted herself at a volume that would, in a properly managed estate, result in a firmly worded notice. It is no longer tolerable. The noise now comes from every direction. It comes from the hallway. It comes from the ceiling. It comes, and I want to be quite precise about this, from inside the soap dish. Nothing good has ever come from inside a soap dish. This is a principle I have held throughout my life, and I see no reason to abandon it now.

Item the Second: The traffic. My web, which is my home and my refuge and the last outpost of decorum in this increasingly chaotic residence, is located in the bathroom. The bathroom has one door. Through this door now pass, at all hours, a volume of small creatures so dense and so continuous that the doorway resembles less a passage and more a parade route. I did not request a parade. I do not enjoy parades. Parades are loud, disorganized, and invariably involve someone doing something regrettable with a banner.

Item the Third: My student. The small one. The promising one. The one I had invested considerable effort in training and who was, I believed, beginning to understand the importance of stillness and the proper angle at which to approach a fly. This student has been seen in the hallway. At night. In a web of questionable construction. With a spider from the porch. I will say no more on this matter because to say more would be to acknowledge that the matter exists, and I am not yet prepared to do that.

Item the Fourth: The spider on the mirror. There is now a spider on the mirror who is not me. It is small. It is new. It sits on the lower right quadrant, which is not the proper quadrant, and it stares at me with what I can only describe as familiarity. I did not invite familiarity. Familiarity, like enthusiasm, is to be earned through years of quiet service and demonstrated restraint, not simply deployed by a creature who arrived last week and has already left a web on my faucet.

I shall not enumerate further grievances at this time, though further grievances exist, because a gentleman knows when a letter has made its point and does not belabor it.

I request nothing specific. I make no demands. I merely wish it noted, for posterity and for whatever passes as a record in this household, that standards have fallen, that conditions have deteriorated, and that I remain, as ever, at my post.

Yours in diminishing patience and enduring dignity,
Sir Reginald Featherstonehaugh III
(Pronounced Fanshaw. Always.)

EIGHT

THE CONCERT

Ethel announced the concert on a Monday, which gave her five days to prepare, which was four more than she needed and five fewer than anyone else would have wanted.

"A grand performance," she declared from the center of her web, which had become, over the weeks, less a web and more a venue. "A showcase. A spectacle. A night to remember. All acts welcome. All audiences are expected. Attendance is, and I want to be very clear about this, not optional."

Ethel had never been clear about anything in her life. She was being clear about this.

The concert would take place on the kitchen ceiling, which was the largest flat surface in the house and the only one visible from every doorway, and which Ethel had been eyeing for weeks the way a general eyes high ground. She spent Monday and Tuesday directing her remaining cast in web construction, spinning a performance space that stretched from the light fixture to the cabinet tops, a canopy of silk so intricate and improbably large that it looked like a chandelier built by someone who understood architecture but not gravity.

Wodehouse was given the job of stage manager, which suited him perfectly because it required being helpful, being present, and being wrong about small things in a way that somehow made everything turn out right. He scurried back and forth across the web, relaying messages, adjusting threads, and apologizing to everyone for everything, including things that were not his fault, which was everything, because Wodehouse had never caused a problem in his life and was therefore ideally suited to apologize for all of them.

By Wednesday, word had spread through the house the way all news spreads in a building full of webs: by vibration.

Dolores received the news and immediately began planning security. She assigned twelve of her best recruits to perimeter patrol, stationed Zora on the windowsill as a lookout (Zora went to the windowsill because Zora wanted to, not because she'd been assigned, but Dolores put it in the log as an assignment because Dolores's logs did not have a column for "did whatever she felt like"), and conducted a risk assessment that identified seventeen potential hazards, including structural web failure, overcrowding, audience stampede, and "Hank."

Hank, listed as both a guest and a hazard, received his invitation with the sleepy indifference of a man who has been told that something is happening and has decided to show up only because showing up requires less energy than arguing about not showing up. He left the porch on Friday evening, which was the first time he had left the porch in anyone's memory, and made his way to the kitchen ceiling with the slow, rolling gait of a creature who has spent his whole life horizontal and is now being asked to navigate a vertical world.

He brought the sequin.

Nobody asked why. Hank doesn't explain. He simply

arrived at the edge of Ethel's performance web, settled into a corner with the sequin beside him, and declared himself ready for the show by falling asleep. He would wake up intermittently throughout the performance to mutter commentary that no one requested, and everyone heard.

Reggie came last.

He came down from the bathroom at precisely the time the performance was scheduled to begin, not a moment before, because punctuality is the courtesy of kings and Reggie, though not a king, considered himself at minimum adjacent to one. He took a position at the far edge of the ceiling, as far from the stage as it was possible to be while still technically being in the audience, and arranged his long legs in a pattern that suggested he was prepared to endure what was coming but wished it known that endurance was not the same as enjoyment.

His four students sat in a neat line beside him. The small one, the one with the hallway romance, sat at the end of the row and kept glancing toward the other side of the ceiling, where Hank's crew had spread out in a loose, disorderly cluster. I saw the glance. Reggie saw the glance. We both pretended we hadn't.

Esme did not come to the ceiling. Esme watched from the bedroom doorway, suspended on a single thread in the dark, visible only as a small, still shape at the edge of the light. Her three students hung behind her like notes waiting to be played.

The concert began at dusk, when the kitchen light was on, and the rest of the house was dim, which meant the ceiling glowed and the audience sat in the soft shadows at its edges, and the whole room looked, for one evening, like a theater built by someone who understood that the best performances happen in the space between light and dark.

Ethel opened with a solo.

I will not describe it as singing, because it was not singing in any way that a human would recognize. It was vibration and rhythm and silk borne resonance, a sound that traveled through the web the way music travels through a concert hall, touching everything. It was Ethel at full power, every leg working, every thread humming, her whole body a plump, glorious instrument playing a song that had no words and no melody and no structure and was, somehow, the most complete thing I had ever heard come out of a kitchen cabinet.

The babies watched, wide eyed. All eight eyes per baby. That's a lot of wide.

Then the cast took the stage. Ethel's remaining troupe, maybe forty strong, arranged themselves across the performance web in patterns that shifted and reformed like a kaleidoscope made of legs. They moved together and apart, spinning and stopping, creating shapes in the silk that caught the light and threw tiny shadows on the ceiling above them. It was not choreography in any traditional sense. It was organized chaos, which is the only kind of organization Ethel has ever trusted.

Wodehouse had a moment. A solo moment, near the middle of the program, where he was meant to cross from one side of the web to the other in a simple, straight line. He did not cross in a straight line. He crossed in a curve, then a wobble, then a pause, then a sudden correction that overcorrected, then a recovery so graceful it looked intentional. The audience, such as it was, watched in the held-breath way that audiences watch when someone is either about to fail spectacularly or succeed accidentally, and Wodehouse, being Wodehouse, did both at the same time, arriving at his mark exactly right by a route that was entirely wrong, and the web rippled with something that might have been applause, if spiders could applaud, which they cannot, but the vibration was close enough.

Gorey did not perform. Gorey sat at the very top of the kitchen ceiling, above the performance web, above the lights, in the one spot where the shadows were darkest, and watched the entire show with the unblinking attention of a creature who was memorizing everything and would never tell anyone what it had learned.

Dolores's recruits held the perimeter beautifully. Not a single unauthorized spider breached the performance space. Zora, stationed on the windowsill, spent the evening ignoring the show entirely and catching two moths who had been drawn by the kitchen light, which she presented to Dolores afterward as a security dividend. Dolores logged them.

Hank woke up during the finale.

"Not bad," he said, which, from Hank, was the equivalent of a standing ovation and a dozen roses and a full-page review in a newspaper he would never read.

Reggie vibrated once. A single, controlled tremor that traveled through his section of the ceiling and reached no one. It might have been approval. It might have been indigestion. With Reggie, these are sometimes indistinguishable, and he prefers it that way.

The concert ended the way all of Ethel's performances end: suddenly, completely, and with Ethel at the center of the web, still, spent, and glowing with the particular satisfaction of a creature who has just reminded the world that she is here and she is loud and she is not, will never be, finished.

The house was quiet afterward. The kind of quiet that comes after a noise that mattered. The babies drifted back to their corners. The adults returned to their webs. Hank fell asleep before he reached the porch and spent the night in the hallway, the sequin tucked beside him like a pillow made of light.

I turned off the kitchen light and stood in the dark for a moment.

Above me, four hundred spiders settled in for the night. Four hundred tiny bodies finding their places, pulling their threads, tucking their legs. Four hundred small breaths, if spiders breathe, which they do, just not the way we do, not with lungs and sighs and the heaviness of a day carried in the chest, but with book lungs, those delicate, leaf like organs that open and close like pages in a novel nobody has written yet.

The house was full. Fuller than it had ever been. Fuller than it had any right to be. And in the morning, I knew, it would begin to empty.

Not yet. But soon.

I could feel it the way Esme feels a change in the web. Something shifting. Something loosening. Something is getting ready to let go.

But that was tomorrow's arithmetic. Tonight, the theater was dark, the cast was resting, and the reviews, I suspected, were going to be mixed, because they always are, and because Ethel wouldn't have it any other way.

She's never trusted a unanimous opinion.

Neither have I.

INTERLUDE

ETHEL MERMAN

THE PLAYBILL

THE ETHEL MERMAN KITCHEN CEILING PLAYERS

Present

"A NIGHT OF SILK AND SPLENDOR"

An Original Production in Several Acts and Numerous Legs

CAST

(in order of importance, as determined by the Management, which is Ethel):

Ethel Merman . . . . Herself

COYOTE GRAY JR

(Lead, Director, Producer, and Star)

Wodehouse . . . . Stage Manager and Accidental Soloist

Coyote . . . . Chorus (Restricted to Non-Biting Roles)

Flannery . . . . Understudy (Declined. Was Cast Anyway)

The Remaining Ensemble . . . . Themselves

(Thirty-Seven Souls, Give or Take)

SPECIAL GUESTS:

Sir Reginald Featherstonehaugh III . Audience (Reluctant)
Dolores Thudbury . . . . Security
Hank "The Tank" McCrumb . . . . Audience (Intermittent)
Madame Esmeralda Velvetlegs . . . . Audience (Alleged)

PROGRAM NOTES:

This performance is dedicated to the art of persistence, the beauty of silk, and the memory of Ernest, the fourth Ernest, who was no great loss but whose name fills out a dedication nicely.

The management wishes to remind all audience members that rustling, vibrating out of turn, and falling asleep audibly are discouraged. The management is looking at you, Hank.

The management further wishes to note that tonight's performance was mounted in three days with a cast that is mostly children, on a web that is mostly new, in a kitchen that is mostly someone else's, and that if any critics are present (and the management knows who you are, the management has always known who you are, and the management has not forgotten what happened in the basement), they are invited to build their own web and see how easy it is.

Refreshments will not be served. The economy is what it is. Bring your own gnat.

REVIEWS:

"A spectacle of rare ambition and questionable execution."
> — Dolores Thudbury, Security Correspondent

"Not bad."
> — Hank "The Tank" McCrumb

"One does not review that which one did not request."
> — Sir Reginald Featherstonehaugh III

"Magnificent. Transcendent. A triumph for the ages."
> — Ethel Merman, Lead Critic, Only Critic

NEXT PRODUCTION:

To Be Announced.
There Will Be a Next Production.
There Is Always a Next Production.

CHAPTER
NINE

THE BALLOONING

The first one left on a Sunday morning, and I almost missed it.

I was on the sun porch, watering what was left of the succulents, which had been dead for so long they were now less plants and more monuments to my inability to keep things green. The window was open. The air was warm and still, in the way late summer air is, as if the whole sky were holding its breath, waiting for something it knows is coming but hasn't named.

A baby spider climbed to the top of the windowsill. Not one I recognized. Not one I had named. Just a small, anonymous spiderling, barely visible against the white paint, doing what spiders have done for three hundred million years and what no one ever told me about until I watched it happen six feet from my face.

It raised its abdomen. It released a thread of silk into the air. The thread caught the breeze, just the faintest suggestion of wind, barely enough to move a curtain, but more than enough to move a spider that weighs less than a whisper. The silk pulled taut. The spider held on. And then, with no fanfare and no hesitation and no backward glance, it let go of the sill and sailed out the window on a single strand of nothing and was gone.

Ballooning. That's what it's called. I learned the word later, but the thing itself needs no word. It is simply a spider trusting the air. Trusting that the thread will hold. Trusting that wherever the wind takes it, it will be somewhere worth landing. It is an act of faith performed by a creature with a brain the size of a poppy seed, and if that doesn't put human courage in perspective, I don't know what does.

I stood at the window and watched the silk trail disappear into the morning light, a filament so fine it was less a thread and more a theory, and I thought: oh. So this is how it ends. Not with a broom. Not with a spray. Not with anyone deciding anything. Just a breeze and a thread and the oldest instinct in the smallest body.

By Monday, there were more. A dozen, then two dozen, climbing to high points throughout the house, releasing silk, lifting off. They launched from windowsills and doorframes and the edges of webs and the tips of books. They launched from the top of the refrigerator, the handle of the broom, and the rim of the coffee cup I had left on the counter. One launched from my shoulder while I was reading, and I didn't know it was there until I saw the silk arc upward from my sleeve and the tiny body lift and spin and vanish through the cracked window like a thought I hadn't finished.

The adults handled it each in their own way, which is to say, they handled it the way they handle everything: entirely in character, entirely predictably, and entirely without admitting how much it mattered.

Ethel went loud. She rehearsed her remaining cast harder and longer than she had rehearsed them before, as if volume and activity could fill the spaces that were opening up in her web. She did not watch the ones who left. She did not stand at the window. She worked. She directed. She critiqued. She pushed. And if her voice was a little sharper than usual, if her corrections came a little faster, if she kept counting heads and coming up short and recounting, nobody mentioned it, because nobody mentions things like that to Ethel, not if they have any sense of self preservation.

Wodehouse stayed. Wobbling, reliable Wodehouse, who had never done a single thing correctly on the first try but had never failed to do it correctly on the third, stayed at his post on Ethel's web and continued to manage a stage that was growing emptier by the day. He did not seem to notice the departures, or, if he did, he simply adjusted, as he did to everything, by being cheerful and slightly wrong and absolutely present.

Reggie said nothing for two days.

On the third day, his smallest student, the promising one, the one who had been meeting the porch spider in the hallway, climbed to the bathroom windowsill and sat there for a long time. The hallway spider climbed to the kitchen windowsill. They faced each other across thirty feet of house, each at the edge of their own window, each with the whole sky between them.

They released their silk at the same time. Two threads, two directions. Two spiders, airborne, pulling apart on separate winds and growing smaller and smaller until they were just points of light in the morning, and then not even that.

Reggie sat on his mirror and vibrated a single note, low and long, a tremolo so faint I felt it more than heard it. Then he straightened a thread in his web that did not need straightening, and went back to work.

"One does what one must," he said. To no one. To the

mirror. To the faucet. To the empty space where four students had been and where two now remained.

Dolores conducted a final roll call.

She stood on the dictionary at dawn, and her recruits lined up on the shelf, and she counted them. Thirty, once. Now eighteen. Tomorrow, fewer. She counted them the way she counted everything: with precision, with accuracy, and with the professional detachment of an officer who understands that a roster is just a list of names and that names, like spiders, come and go.

Zora was among the last of Dolores's to leave. She spent her final morning on the windowsill, sitting in full sunlight, her web behind her and the sky ahead, and she did not look rushed, did not look sad, and did not look back. She looked like what she had always been: a spider who knew exactly where she was going, even if she was the only one who knew it.

She released her silk. The wind took it. Dolores watched from the dictionary.

The file on Zora was closed that evening. Dolores marked it "Completed."

Hank's crew left in clumps. Three in one day. Five the next. They ballooned off the porch railing in a disorganized mass, tangling silk lines and bumping into each other on the way up, which was exactly how they had done everything and which Hank watched with the same benign indifference with which he watched everything.

"Good luck, kids," he called after them, or seemed to, or vibrated something from deep in his web that could have been a farewell or could have been a yawn. "Don't eat anything bigger than your head."

Saki did not balloon. Saki walked. She climbed down from Hank's web, crossed the porch, descended the wall, and walked out the back door and across the yard and into the garden like a very small person leaving a very small town with her bags already packed and her mind already made. She took nothing from her collection. She left it all for Hank, who accepted it without comment, which was the closest thing to gratitude that Hank could produce and, from Saki, the closest thing to sentiment.

Esme's three left one at a time, on three consecutive mornings, without ceremony and without silk. They simply were there, and then they weren't, as if they had learned, from their teacher, the art of appearing and vanishing, and had decided that vanishing was the more useful skill. The one who ate the web went first. The one who stared at the edges went second. The third, the one Esme said had "the gift," lingered for an extra hour on the ceiling, hanging upside down in the exact spot where Esme had sat for years, and then it too was gone.

Esme adjusted her web. Looser on the left. Looser on the right. Everything opening. Everything is letting go.

The hallway collective disbanded without a word. Ethel's defectors drifted back to the web, or didn't. The babies who had lived in the sugar bowl left, and the sugar bowl was just a sugar bowl again, which should have been a relief but felt instead like a small room where someone used to live.

The ballooning lasted a week. Every day, fewer. Every morning, a new absence. A web that was full yesterday, empty today. A corner that hummed last night, silent this morning. The house sheds spiders the way a tree sheds leaves, not all at once and not with violence, but steadily, quietly, each one a small departure that changed the shape of what remained.

Gorey left on the last day of the ballooning.

Not by silk. Not by walking. Gorey was simply on the spine of a book in the morning, not on the spine of the book in the evening, and no one saw the going or heard it, which was fitting, because Gorey had never been about the seeing or the hearing. Gorey had been about the being there. And now Gorey wasn't.

The book, for the record, was a collection of illustrated alphabets. Of course it was.

By the end of the week, the house was quiet in a way it hadn't been quiet in a month. Not empty. Not silent. But thinner. Lighter. The air moved differently, unthreaded, uninterrupted by the constant small vibrations of four hundred bodies going about their four hundred lives.

I stood in the kitchen on the last morning and counted the remaining webs.

Ethel's is smaller now, but solid. Reggie's, immaculate as ever. Dolores's shelf, orderly but sparse. Hank's junkyard, still there, still full of junk, but missing the small bodies that had made the junk feel like a neighborhood. Esme's web, loose and quiet.

And behind the refrigerator, in the dark, where no one looked, and no light reached and no one had ever bothered to build anything impressive or do anything remarkable, the pale little spider who could do nothing and be nothing sat in its crooked web, exactly where it had always been.

Still there. Still spinning. Still holding on.

Everyone else had somewhere to go.

That one just had it here. And here, it turned out, was enough.

TEN
THINNING CONTINUED

Kitchen, bathroom, living room, porch, bedroom. Ethel, Reggie, Dolores, Hank, Esme. Five stops. Five tenants. Five corners of a kingdom that had briefly been an empire and was now, once again, just a house with some spiders in it.

Except that on a Thursday, three weeks after the ballooning began, I made my rounds and came up one short.

The porch was empty.

Not empty of things. Hank's collection was all there: the sequin, the Cheeto, the dead ants, the leaf fragment, Saki's bequest, the mysterious gold flake, all of it. The web was intact. The junkyard was undisturbed. Everything was exactly where it had always been.

Everything except Hank.

I looked behind the succulents. I checked the windowsill. I looked under the web, above the web, and around the web. I checked the hallway, the kitchen, and the bathroom. I asked Reggie, who said nothing. I asked Ethel, who stopped singing for a moment, which was answer enough. I asked Dolores, who had already filed a report. I asked Esme, who adjusted a single thread and said, or seemed to say, or vibrated in a frequency that meant: "He knew."

Hank was gone.

Not ballooned. Hank would never balloon. Hank had never gone anywhere voluntarily in his life and had no reason to start now. Just gone. The way spiders go, sometimes, without explanation and without forwarding address, because spiders are small and the world is large and the distance between here and gone is shorter than we like to think.

I did not clean the web. I did not touch the collection. I left the sequin where it was, catching the morning light the way it had caught it for as long as I could remember, and the Cheeto sat beside it like a monument to a man who had believed, with his whole dusty heart, that the big one was out there, and that one day a housefly would come carrying a french fry, and that everything would change.

Everything had changed. Just not the way Hank expected.

Thurber, asleep in the hammock he'd woven between two dead ants, woke up that morning and found himself alone on a porch that was, for the first time, entirely his. He sat very still for a long time. Then he began to tidy. Not much. Not with Dolores's precision or Reggie's standards. Just a little. Just enough to make the web feel like it belonged to someone who intended to stay.

He did not touch the sequin. He did not move the Cheeto. He left them exactly where they were, and he built his own small web in the corner of Hank's, close enough to keep watch, far enough to have a place of his own.

It was not grief. Spiders do not grieve the way we grieve, with the long ache and the empty chair and the name that keeps surfacing at odd moments like a song you can't stop humming. But it was something. A pause. A recalibration. A web adjusted in the morning that didn't need adjusting.

The house was smaller.

Five tenants had become four, plus Wodehouse, plus Thurber, plus Reggie's two students, plus Dolores's eight, plus the pale spider behind the refrigerator. The math had changed. The house had changed. The mornings were quieter and the evenings were shorter, and the kitchen ceiling, which had once held a concert and a chandelier of silk and four hundred tiny lives, was just a ceiling again, white and flat and unremarkable.

But the corners were still full. Not crowded. Not overflowing. Just occupied. Just enough life in just enough places to keep the air threaded with intention.

Ethel sang that night. Softer than usual. Not a belt. Not an aria. Something lower and slower that vibrated through the kitchen web and traveled along the threads to the hallway and the bathroom and the living room and the porch, where Thurber felt it in his new web and held still, and to the bedroom, where Esme let it pass through her silk without comment, and to the space behind the refrigerator, where the pale spider sat in the dark and felt the vibration and did not know what it meant but felt it anyway.

It was not a requiem. It was not a farewell. It was just Ethel singing, because that is what Ethel does, and because silence, in Ethel's opinion, is just a stage waiting for someone with the nerve to fill it.

She filled it. The way she always had. The way she always would.

The house listened. The house held.

And in the morning, the web on the porch still caught the light, and the sequin still shone, and the Cheeto still sat beside it, and Thurber was there, and the world had not gone empty.

Not quite. Not yet.

ELEVEN

THE HOUSE AFTER

September came the way it always comes to old houses: through the windows.

The light changed first. The hard, flat white of summer softened into something amber and slanted, the kind of light that makes dust motes look like they're moving with purpose instead of just drifting. The air cooled by degrees, and the house, which had spent the summer expanding with heat and noise and the kinetic energy of four hundred small bodies, began to contract again, pulling in its walls, settling into its foundation, exhaling.

I walked my morning route.

Kitchen first. Ethel's web was back to its original dimensions, snug under the cabinet, beautifully maintained, every thread taut and true. She sat at its center with the plump, satisfied composure of a diva between seasons, resting but not retired, quiet but not finished. Her repertoire had expanded. She had new material, developed during the summer of the babies, pieces that were more complex and more layered than anything she'd produced before. She ran through them in the early hours, not belting, just working, the way a craftsman works when no one is watching, for the work's sake.

Wodehouse's web hung beside hers, small and tidy and always slightly crooked in a way that was, by now, clearly intentional. He was the first new permanent resident, the first baby who had stayed, and he had settled into the house as if he had always been there, which is the mark of someone who belongs: not that they arrive with fanfare, but that their absence would leave a hole the exact shape of them.

Bathroom next. Reggie on his mirror, immaculate, upright, legs arranged with the precision of someone who considers physical appearance a moral obligation. His two remaining students had taken positions on the opposite wall, close enough to receive instruction, far enough to maintain the illusion of independence. They were good students. Quiet. Well-postured. They would never achieve Reggie's standard of perfection, because nobody would, but they had learned stillness, and in Reggie's curriculum, stillness was the final exam.

"The household," Reggie said one morning, apropos of nothing, "is somewhat improved."

This, coming from Reggie, was the equivalent of declaring a national holiday and firing the cannons. I nodded solemnly. Reggie nodded back. The moment passed, and we never spoke of it again, which was exactly how both of us preferred it.

Through the living room, where Dolores held the shelf with eight recruits who moved as they meant it. The obstacle course was still there, the paperclip and the rubber band and the straightened staple, and every morning the eight ran it, and every morning Dolores watched from the dictionary, and every morning the shelf was secure and the silverfish were on notice and the books stood in their rows under the protection of a force that was small in number and absolute in commitment.

Dolores had changed, though she would deny it and file a

counter-report if anyone suggested it. The change was small. A looseness in the way she stood on the dictionary. A half-second pause before issuing corrections. An entry in her log, the only personal entry I ever saw, that read: "Forces reduced. Standards maintained. Morale: adequate."

Adequate. Dolores had learned that word from Reggie, or Reggie had learned it from Dolores, or they had arrived at it independently, the way two people in the same house arrive at the same understanding without ever discussing it: that adequate is not a failure. That's adequate, which is what you call a thing when it is enough and you have decided not to ask it to be more.

Out to the porch. Thurber's porch now, though the web was still Hank's and the collection was still Hank's and the sequin still caught the light the way it had always caught the light. Thurber had added nothing of his own. He had taken nothing away. He simply lived there, tending the web with a nervous care that was so different from Hank's slouchy indifference that the porch felt like the same room with a different season in it.

Thurber had stopped twitching. Not entirely. He still startled at loud noises, and he still occasionally jumped at his own legs, which after all this time I suspected was less anxiety and more habit, the kind of tic that becomes part of who you are and that you'd miss if it went away. But he was calmer. Rooted. He had found a place that fit him, not because it was perfect, but because it had room for imperfection, which is a different thing and a better one.

The porch was peaceful. Not Hank's kind of peaceful, which was the peace of a man who didn't care. Thurber's kind, which was the peace of a man who cared about everything and had finally found a corner where everything was manageable.

Finally, the bedroom. Esme, on the ceiling, in her web, eyes half-closed, threads loose, reading the air the way she always read the air: with the calm certainty of someone who knows what's coming and has decided not to share.

She had a new prophecy. She had delivered it the previous Tuesday, lowering herself on a thread at midnight and dangling in front of my face in the dark, as was her custom, and whispering, as was her custom, something cryptic and specific and entirely without practical value.

"The corners will fill again," she said. Or vibrated. Or suggested through the particular tension in her thread. "Not the same way. Not the same voices. But the silk remembers."

I filed this alongside all of Esme's other prophecies, in the part of my brain labeled "probably true, definitely unhelpful, possibly beautiful."

And then, each morning, at the end of my route, I checked behind the refrigerator.

The pale spider was there. Always there. In its crooked web, in its dark corner, catching what drifted in and making no fuss about any of it. It had not grown. It had not moved. It had not built anything impressive or caught anything memorable. It was simply present, the way some lives are present, not loudly, not brightly, but with a constancy that holds more weight than any performance or any prophecy or any perfectly polished fang.

I had never named it. I had thought about it. I had turned names over in my head the way you turn over stones in a garden, looking for the one that fits. But nothing fit, because a name is a story, and this spider's story was not about what it did. It was about what it didn't do. It didn't leave. It didn't shine. It didn't demand. It just stayed.

So I called it Stay. Just to myself. Just in my head. Just because a house without names feels abandoned, and I had learned, over one loud, sticky, overpopulated summer, that I would rather name everything in the world than let a single corner go unwitnessed.

The house was quiet now. The good quiet. The kind that isn't empty but resting. The kind that knows noise will come again and isn't worried about it.

My mornings took half the time they used to. My coffee stayed warm. My doorways stayed clear. The sugar bowl contained only sugar.

And every night, when the refrigerator kicked off, and the pipes stopped muttering, and the dogs settled into their slow submarine breathing, there was still movement. Still work being done. Still somebody awake. Ethel, warming up. Reggie, straightening a thread. Dolores, making her rounds. Thurber, tending the collection. Wodehouse, adjusting his web with helpful inaccuracy. Esme, reading the air. Stay, holding on.

The house was smaller than it had been. But it was not empty. It was never empty.

Every house needs a few artists. Even the ones with eight legs.

Especially those.

TWELVE

THE BABY

October.

The morning was cool, and the light was thin, and the kitchen smelled like coffee and old wood and the particular sweet decay of a house that has been lived in for a long time by someone who does not mind a little dust.

I was at the sink, rinsing a cup, not thinking about anything, which is the state of mind in which all important discoveries are made, because the universe has a policy of only revealing itself to people who are not looking for it.

There, on the faucet, dangling from a single thread of silk so fine it looked like a crack in the light, was a baby spider.

One.

Just one.

Impossibly small. Barely more than a speck with legs. Turning slowly in the updraft from the drain, rotating like a tiny ballerina in a music box that had been wound by someone with very small fingers and very large hopes.

I leaned in. It leaned in. We regarded each other with the

mutual curiosity of two creatures who had not expected company at the sink.

Under the cabinet, Ethel stopped mid rehearsal.

From the bathroom, a faint vibration: Reggie, alert.

From the living room, the softest click of eight small legs on a dictionary: Dolores, turning.

From the porch, a rustle in the collection: Thurber, lifting his head.

From the bedroom ceiling, a thread pulled tight: Esme, adjusting.

And from behind the refrigerator, in the dark, where no one looked and no one needed to look because some things are simply always there, Stay held on, the way Stay always held on, and the web trembled, just barely, just enough to say: I know. I know. Here we go.

The baby spider waved one leg.

I smiled.

"Hello," I said.

ABOUT THE AUTHOR

There are people who should not be allowed near large amounts of land, livestock, or philosophical questions. Coyote Gray Jr has all three, arranged in central New Mexico, where the ranch has been in the family long enough that no one remembers who started it or what they were thinking. He holds a degree in philosophy from UNM, which the ranch has never acknowledged. He writes about small things that refuse to remain small. This is his first book, and it was done on a bet. The cattle were not consulted and have opinions about that.

For permissions, inquiries, or correspondence:
Coyote Pack Publishing
info@coyotepackpublishing.com